Charlie

This crocodile belongs to:

Charlie

For snappy dressers and jazz lovers everywhere – G. D.

To Triana Grafiá Gonzales – A. B.

First published in the United Kingdom in 2023 by
Thames & Hudson Ltd, 181A High Holborn, London WC1V 7QX

This paperback edition published in 2024

If I had a crocodile © 2023 and 2024 Thames &
Hudson Ltd, London
Text © 2023 Gabby Dawnay
Illustrations © 2023 Alex Barrow

British Library Cataloguing-
in-Publication Data
A catalogue record for this
book is available from
the British Library

ISBN 978-0-500-66027-0

Printed and bound in China
by Everbest Printing Co. Ltd

MIX
From responsible
sources
FSC® C124385
FSC
www.fsc.org

Be the first to know about our new releases,
exclusive content and author events by visiting
thamesandhudson.com
thamesandhudsonusa.com
thamesandhudson.com.au

If I had a crocodile

GABBY DAWNAY   ALEX BARROW

I do like ,

I'd love a   ,

and   are pretty smooth...

but I'd prefer a *snappy* pet
to help me find my groove.

What about some sort of bird –

a   or a   ?

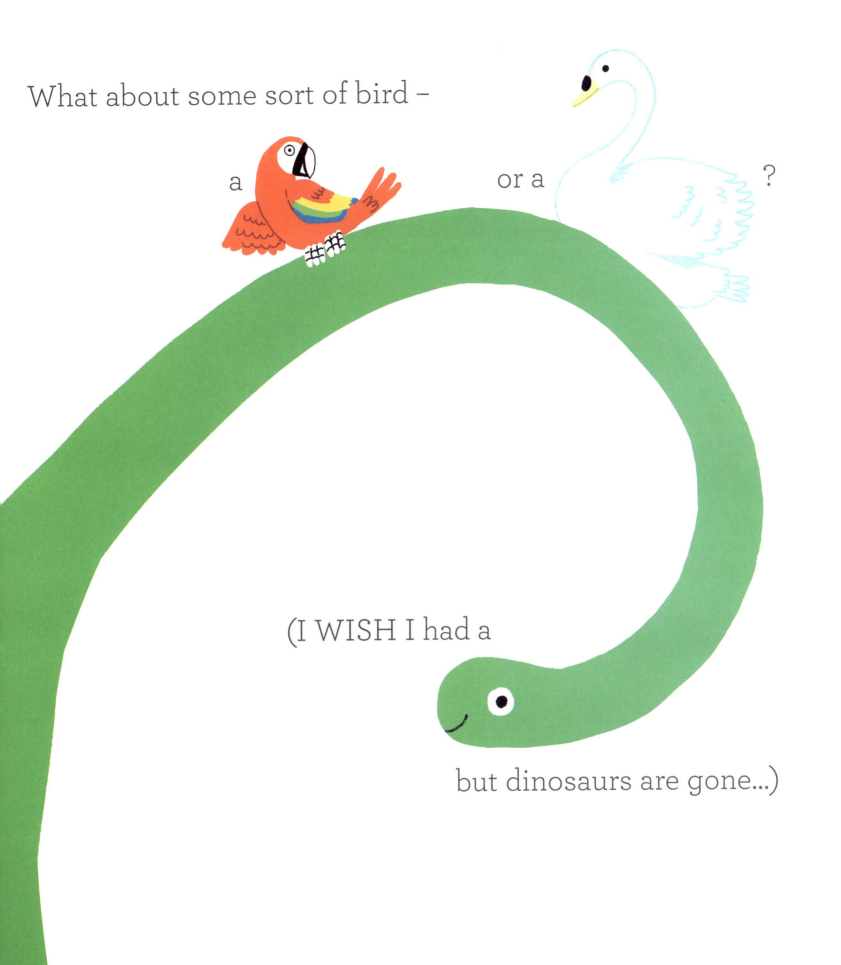

(I WISH I had a

but dinosaurs are gone...)

I really want a sassy pet,
a pet that makes me smile –
the kind of pet that has pizzazz
and lots and lots of style.

Oh, if I had a

CROCODILE...

I'd take him for a stroll.
We wouldn't need to hurry,
'cause that's just the way we roll.

Crocodiles are groovy –
they're a jazzy kind of pet.

So when we got to school each day
we'd practise clarinet.

THE
COUNT
SNAPPY
QUINTET

Crocodiles have lovely skin,
it's waterproof and bumpy.
But NEVER poke them with a stick
in case it makes them grumpy.

Whenever people ask me
why I want a crocodile,
I look them in the eye and say,
'I like the way they *smile*...'

I'd teach my crocodile to play
my favourite game of...

SNAP!

And if he won I know my friends
would shout 'Hooray!' and clap.

Crocodiles are cool but kind,
as well as very strong.
So when I go to ballet class
I know he'd tag along.

I would take him boating,
and we'd watch the world go past...
for crocodiles love floating,
though they swim extremely fast!

I'd always buy his dinner
from the butcher down the street.

For crocodiles are carnivores,
and carnivores eat meat.

Crocodiles are sensitive
and here's the reason why:
each time they eat their dinner
I have noticed that they CRY!

Their jaws are super powerful
but strangely cannot chew.
They swallow food completely whole
so watch out for the...

...!

Crocodiles are sometimes cross
but my one would be tame,
especially after dinner
when we'd play another game.

Then my pet would have a nap –
I wonder if he'd snore?
Relaxing on the sofa
like a living dinosaur!

Crocodiles have mighty fangs –
the most you've ever seen!
So every night I'd help my croc
to scrub-a-dub them clean.

My snappy chap would stay with me
for many, many years –
we'd have the BEST adventures
(and we'd shed a lot of tears).

However far he wandered
or wherever he might roam,
my crocodile would use his heart
to find his way back home...

Meet the creators of the series

Gabby Dawnay is a writer and poet. She is a regular contributor to *OKIDO* magazine and a script-writer for children's television.

Alex Barrow is a London-based illustrator and musician. He is the art director for and a regular contributor to *OKIDO* magazine.

Together Gabby and Alex are the duo behind the bestselling *If I had a* series, as well as numerous other children's books including *A House for Mouse* and *A Song for Bear* (both Thames & Hudson) and the Kate Greenaway-nominated *A Possum's Tail* (Tate Publishing).